I'M BORED' by author Kenneth J. Sousa flaunts his literary originality creating this masterpiece tale of a few days in the life of a dog, as told by the dog himself. The story is terrifically layered with adventure, excitement, cunning manipulative dog-thinking, and a few well-done illustrations to top off the story allowing readers to better visualize the characters and events. Plus, it may just keep a child from thinking "the grass is greener outside of the house," if he or she becomes bored themselves.

—Beth Adams: *Hollywood Book Reviews*

Here is a children's book, suitable for kids of all ages, a book illuminating and fun for adults as well. I'm Bored captures the vernacular at the source: out of the mouth of a dog. The canine outlook has a great deal to recommend it; who among us hasn't wanted to know what their pet really thinks? This canny book will broaden perspectives and help set all breeds, human and otherwise, free.

—David Allen: *Pacific Book Review*

I'M BORED

KENNETH J SOUSA

ISBN 978-1-64133-777-9 (softcover)
ISBN 978-1-64133-779-3 (hardcover)
ISBN 978-1-64133-778-6 (ebook)

Printed in the United States of America.

Brilliant Books Literary
137 Forest Park Lane Thomasville
North Carolina 27360 USA

I'M BORED

Every day's the same. I wake up, they feed me, and then it's outside to the fenced in patio where I bake all summer and freeze all winter. Sure, there's a doghouse, but did you ever sleep in one of those things? The door is always open, mice use it as a gymnasium and there are more fleas than Barnum and Bailey's. Do they care?

I guess I shouldn't complain. I get two 'squares' a day and they do let me in at night. Although that's to protect their precious possessions. Ha, they've got to be kidding if they think I'm going to take a kick in the chops just so they won't miss a night in front of that noisy box. As far as I'm concerned, if a few barks don't get rid of a burglar, he can take the place. A couple of meals a day isn't worth getting killed over.

Speaking of meals, I'd like to sink my teeth into that pesky cat next door. She spends half her day figuring out ways to drive me crazy. Like jumping on the dog house when I'm trying to sleep or slinking so close to the fence that my teeth almost reach her whiskers and my face ends up looking like a quilt.

Just once I'd like to get over the fence; out into the world, freedom of the open road, other dogs to play with, cats to chase and a million garbage cans at my disposal. I know, I get to see it twice a year when they bring me to the man in the white jacket who forces open my mouth and sticks me with sharp things. There's another one I would like to sink my teeth into.

Oh oh, here comes trouble! It's the man who comes to look at the glass bowl on the side of the house. He always uses the back gate but closes it so I won't escape.

I remember the first time he came; it was shortly after I had moved here. One day this uniformed man opened the gate and waltzed right in. Well, this was my chance to show the family I'm a great watchdog. I went straight for his pant leg. Of course I wasn't going to do any serious damage, just a little nip and tug to show I meant business. Anyway, this guy pulls out a can and sprays me right in the kisser! I couldn't believe such pain could come from the press of a finger. My eyes stung, my nose burned and I ran into the side of the doghouse trying to get back in! And that's not all, when the Mrs. heard the commotion she came running out but instead of yelling at the man who damaged her pet, she yelled and called me that awful word, "bad-dog." And these are the people who expect me to take a chunk out of a leg coming through an open window? Do they care?

Wait a minute, it's not the usual man coming through the gate, and it's a woman! I'm not going to bark and if I squeeze as far back into the house as I can, maybe she won't see me. If she doesn't see me, maybe she'll leave the gate open.

She's lifting the latch. She must be related to the man, she has the same uniform along with that awful can sticking out of her pocket. She's walking through the gate. Will she see me and close it? She's taking a quick look around the yard. Gee, if I squeeze back any further in this piece of junk my tail will break through. She doesn't see me! She's leaving the gate open! Calm down, calm down. As soon as she gets by me I'm going to make a break for it. That's it, only a little further, hold my breath. She's by! Ok, run for the gate, run run! What's that sound? It's the Mrs. calling. Pretend I don't hear. Run! Here she comes! Only a few more steps! I made it! I'm free! Keep running, she'll never catch me now!

"Hoooooonnnnnnkkkkkk!!!"

Phew, that was close, only a few seconds of freedom and it almost ends under a truck. But who cares, I made it! Look, I can run as far and as fast as I want. There are no fences and no one to make me do tricks for dry tasteless biscuits. And the cats, wait till I get hold of my first cat.

There's one now, a calico. This is going to be fun. "Roof roof," run you son of a sea lion, I'm going to chase you until your legs fall off! "Roof roof," I almost gotcha. Oh no, she ran up a tree. Come down you chicken, play fair! Shucks, it looks like she's gonna stay up there all day. I can't hang around here, there are places to go, things to see.

Speaking of things to see, check out that poodle across the street. Vah vah vah voom. I've got to get a closer look at this dish.

"Beeeeeeep!"

Oop, I keep forgetting about the traffic out here. Got to keep my eyes and ears open. Now, where did that poodle go? Ah, there she is ducking around the corner of that building. Looks like she wants to play hard to get. Well, she'll have to play a lot harder to get away from this boy.

"Roof roof," wait up. Only a few more strides and I'll be around the corner with my true love. Ain't life wonderful?

"Grrrrrrrrr!"

It's a Doberman! Hold it boy; I didn't know she belonged to you. Honest I didn't. See, I'm going. Now put away those teeth, I'm going, see. Bye bye.

Paws don't fail me now! Is he following? I don't dare look. Just in case I'll duck under this car, then into the alley, now under this fence and across another street to those woods.

Made it! Phew, close again. Hey there's a gray bushy tail, get him! "Roof."

There's another! "Roof roof." This is great. I could do this forever. "Roof roof......"

Guess I showed them who's boss of these woods. These woods, these woods, hmmmmm, which way did I come in here? Let's see, I chased the first bushy tail this way. No, it was that way. No no, that was the second one, or was it the third? Who cares, I am as free as a bird and can go in any direction I want. There's no place I have to be and no one I have to please. I only hope I run into some water soon, cause being free sure makes a dog thirsty.

Hey, there's another cat. This one is black with a long white stripe down its back. I'll make short work of him. "Roof roof roof," he ran into a thicket, I got him now!

"Sssssssshhhhhhhhh."

Ughaaaaaaa, that cat sprayed me and it makes my nose run and my eyes burn like the spray from the uniform guy. Let me out of here! Run run! I'm running as fast as I can but still can't get away from that smell. Got to rest, can't rest, got to get away from that smell. There's a stream, jump in quick!

* * *

Mmmmmm that water tastes good and I can't see that strange cat following me, he must be afraid of the water. I guess it's safe to come out now. Oh no, the smell is still here. The smell is on me!

"Splassshhh." I'm going to stay in this water until that stuff is all gone, even if it takes all night. Speaking of all night, these woods are getting dark and this water's getting awfully cold. Where am I going to sleep tonight? When am I going to get fed?

Aw, I don't have to worry about being fed; there must be a million things to eat in these woods. Besides, tomorrow I'll find my way out and every garbage pail in the world will be waiting to be emptied. My mouth waters just thinking about it. At any rate I have to get out of this water, I'm freezing to death.

Brrrrr, I didn't think it got this cold out at night. Anyway, let me sniff around and see what I can find to eat. "Sniff sniff," can't find anything here, but there are those little round things I see the bushy tails eat. Let me try one....Yuck, those things are terrible, even dog biscuits taste better than that. Let me sniff some more.

* * *

"Sniff sniff sniff," it seems like I've been sniffing forever, its real dark now and all I smell is that horrible stuff that strange cat sprayed. Got to get some rest, I'm hungry, but if I don't get some sleep I'll fall down from exhaustion anyway. Besides, I can last till morning when I'll find all those delicious trashcans.

Under this tree seems like a good place to camp out, nice soft leaves, even a few pine needles, they kind of help hide the smell. Gee it's dark out there.

"Rustle rustle."

What's that! "Roof roof," who's out there? "Roof roof roof."

"Rustle."

"Roof roof roof......"

* * *

At last, the sun's coming up, but I don't think I slept a wink all night. Every time I moved a pine needle stuck me, mosquitoes used my nose for blood transfusions and something kept running through the bushes. Then every time I barked, " who's there," a stupid thing in a tree repeated the question, "who who who."

I'm starved, got to sniff my way out of these woods. On second thought, I better not do too much sniffing, this smell is killing me. But anyway, I'm alive, fairly well, and ready to explore my second day of freedom. Let me see, I think I'll try this way.

* * *

This couldn't be the way; I've been traveling for miles and have found only woods woods woods. Wait a minute, what's that sound? It's a whoosh, and there's another whoosh. That's the sound of speeding cars. It must be a road, and where there are roads there are houses and where there are houses, there are garbage cans!

* * *

Found a road but I've been walking forever. Can't cross it cause the traffic's so heavy but if I don't find food soon I'm going to collapse. Hold it, what's that up ahead? It's a big black air creature picking at something on the roadside. Maybe I've found breakfast.

"Roof," fly away. Good, now let me see, what have we here? The thing is so squashed I can hardly tell. Sniifff, uuuughhhaaa, it's that horrible smell! It's one of those striped cats that sprayed me. Let me out of here!

* * *

How long have I been walking? It seems like ages. The sun's going down and still I haven't found an end to this road. Well at least there's a stream running beside it so I haven't been thirsty but it is getting dark and I'll have to go into the woods to sleep soon. I don't think it's safe by the road at night. There's a good spot, near those bushes by the rock.

Not a bad place, and I made it just as it was getting real dark. What's that noise! "Roof roof roof roof......."

* * *

Another sleepless night, half the morning on the road, and I can't remember the last time I ate. And the cars, the cars keep zoom zoom zooming by. Look the line of traffic, it never ends. "Zoom zoom," wait, that one's not zooming, it's slowing down, so is the one behind it. They're turning in at a building with a big orange roof. "Sniffff," what's that smell? It's food, food, I'm saved!

I can't wait, only a little further and I'll be at the source of that beautiful smell. The aroma's coming from the back. I was right. I hit the jackpot! This place is a gold mine of garbage cans. Let me at em!

Which one first? This one smells good. Oh yes, meat, and leftover potatoes..... Mmmmm, that was good, lets try the next one. Chicken bones, my favorite, they're even covered with gravy. I only wish there weren't so tiny winged things landing on them, but they're great anyway. Mmmmm Mmmmmmm.....

"Hey you! Yah you, the mangy mutt. Get out of that trash! Scram!"

Ouch! You don't have to kick me. I'm going. Just give me time to look in this other barrel. Ouch. I'm going. I'm going.

"And you stink too dog. Why don't you go find your owner and tell him to give you a bath!"

I stink; he should talk with those hairy armpits. Duck! He's throwing rocks. I better make a run for it. There's another road, and it leads to houses. And there's a cat, not a fake one either. "Roof roof roof!"

Hey this cat must be dumb, it's not even running away. This'll be easy pickings. I'll finally get to sink my teeth into some feline flesh. Oh oh, it got its back up and it's hissing. Well a little hissing isn't going to stop this dog.

"Eeeeeeeeee! Eeeeeeeee! Eeeee!" It slashed my nose! I'm bleeding, my nose is bleeding! She's going to do it again! Run run!

Look, there's a bunch of dogs, I'll join them. Strength in numbers. We'll come back and eat that cat alive.

"Roof roof roof," hey fellas, you should've seen the dirty trick some cat pulled on me. She's down the street; if we hurry we can still catch her.

"Ssssnnnniffff ssssnnniffff, sniff sniff sniff."

Hey fellas where you running to? Come back, don't you want to help me get the cat? Come back! "Roof roof."

They must be a bunch of chickens. One sniff of danger and they take off. Well I'll just find some other dogs who'll show a little more guts. Ooooo, speaking of guts, mine are full of pain. There's a grassy spot over there..... Ahaaa, that's better. Now to find some tough dogs.

"Ooooooo," those pains again. Must be from the chicken bones I ate. Some of those little flying things looked sick too. There's some more grass. Oooooo, when are the pains going to stop? "Oooooooooo……..."

* * *

"Roof roof roof….." Another night in the woods, but at least the pains are gone. Two whole days of agony. I never thought they would stop. Now I'm starving to death again. Got to find another barrel, but this time I'm staying away from chicken bones.

I better get started. I don't know how long it will take to find a meal, and I went pretty far into the woods last night. Hold it, there's a road right over there. Looks like today is going to be my lucky day. I'll say it is, there's a whole pack of dogs rummaging through some cans behind that big building with the buses in front.

"Roof roof," make some room for me. Hey, wait, you don't have to take off and leave all this. I'd be glad to share. Aw, who cares, let them run, all the more for me.

Let's see, I'll tackle this big can first. Oh oh, just paper and broken pencils, maybe the next one will have more. Nope, and not in the next one either. It looks as if those other dogs picked them clean.

Hungry again, and alone, why won't any of the other dogs have anything to do with me? Maybe it wasn't so bad being fenced in all day after all. I could go for a nice bowl of food and a quiet nap in the old doghouse. I wish I could find my way back.

"Get out of here you smelly dog!"

Run; don't want to be pelted with rocks again. Watch out for that truck with the cage on back, it almost hit me. It's slowing down, it's stopped, a man is getting out. Better be careful, it looks like he might have a rock in his hand. No, it's a biscuit and he's calling me over. See, I knew things would pick up.

Mmmmmm that biscuit tastes good.

Look out! He's swinging something over me! It's a net! Try to bite through! I can't, I'm stuck. "Roof roof roof roof......"

* * *

They've got me shut up in a cage. It's in a room with rows of cages and there's other dogs here too. At any rate it's warm, and they do feed me. But still, there's something funny going on in this place.

When I woke up this morning there was a whole pack of dogs in the cages and now there's only a few. It seems that every so often the door opens and a man comes in. See, here he comes now. I almost know the routine by heart and I'm getting a little worried. He's going to take that dog with the black patch over his eye to the table in the corner and strap him down. Next comes the worst part, the part with the needle. He's going to stick the dog with the needle and the dog will fall asleep. Only even when the man lifts the dog to carry it out, the dog won't wake up. See what I mean.

* * *

Oh oh, the door's opening again, he's coming to get the dog next to me. Yup, the same routine. Up on the table, strapped down, stuck with the needle, unstrapped and carried out the door. There's only one left now.

How much longer do I have before he comes for me? How long before I get put on the table and strapped down? How long before I get the needle! Calm down, calm down, none of the other dogs made a fuss, none of the other dogs cried. It won't hurt; they're only going to put me to sleep.

Oh oh, I hear footsteps. They're stopping at the door. The doorknob's turning. That ugly man couldn't be coming for me. I'm not tired. I don't want to go to sleep. The door's opening. No no, "roof roof roof."

Wait, it's different this time. There are two people coming through the door. Maybe they're bringing in other dogs. Maybe they'll be ahead of me.

Who's that other person? It's not a man, it's a woman. It's a woman and it's the Mrs! It's the Mrs. and she's come to get me. Yes, they are opening the cage. She's come to get me! She does care! She's trying to get the leash on my collar but she's having a hard time doing it because she's holding her nose at the same time. She did it, she got it on and she's bringing me out to the car. Oh oh, she's dumping me in the back and she's still holding her nose. She must think I stink! But at least I'm going home.

Oh no, we're stopping at the place with the white coats, but it's not that time. Wait. Don't throw me in that big tub full of red stuff. It looks like blood. No no, I don't want to go in, aauuughhh! Wait a minute, it's not blood, and it's juice from those red things that grow in the back yard. The things with the green vines and strings I always get caught up in. They're drowning me in it. Stop! Stop! I hate it. "Roof roof roof....."

* * *

Back in the car and I get to sit up front. The Mrs. isn't even holding her nose. And look, we're home already; I couldn't have been that far away. Is she going to take me in the house? No, she's taking me around to the back gate.

I'm in, and there's a big bowl of food waiting for me. Mmmmm was that good. Too bad it's gone already. There's the cat.

"Roof," hi cat. The doghouse, the old dog house, they cleaned it up and even painted it, and the mice are gone. Think I'll just stretch out on the patio a bit. Naaa, this isn't too comfortable. I'll lie near the fence and watch the cars. It feels so good to be home. I guess they do care.

DOG
WELCOME HOME

I
was
born
in the
spring
of 1953.
Few heralded
my coming
and fewer
wanted anything
to do with me
once I arrived.
You see my lineage
was of question.
Father was a Scot
from Pine Woods, and
mother was a Norwegian
from Spruce Hill. It was a
wild quick affair, the kind
often inspired by warm summer
breezes. From the creator's love
came what you see standing here now.
It hasn't really been an easy life:
I have the beauty of my mother and the
strength of my father, but was constantly
berated by my peers for having odd looking
appendages and a different color. At first I
didn't let it bother me, but year after year
I noticed that others were being chosen. I began
to find fault in myself. I stooped and drooped and
I almost never stood up straight. By this time the
only thing I figured I was good for was to feed some
demon hellfire. Actually I felt I was already living it.
One day when I knew I couldn't exist a second longer,
a little bird landed on my shoulder and hopped to my ear
and said, "Pal, you want to know what your problem is: you
think you are sick, old and dead, therefore you act sick, old
and dead. Pick up those shoulders, suck in that mid-section.
Smile. Now look at yourself. You're a beautiful living
creation!" So I looked and I was! And the very
next day you came along. I stood
up straight and tall, just
loving to be alive.
It was love at first sight: I love you and you love me.
And now I'll be what I should be, a tall and beautiful Christmas Tree.

KEN'S BRIEF WRITING AUTOBIOGRAPHY

Kenneth J. Sousa was born on March 20, 1947. He is the oldest of 10 children. He began getting up and writing down his dreams in High School. He also received an A in creative writing class. He received three scholarships upon graduation and attended Bridgewater State Teachers College in 1965 but left after failing Math. In 1966 he entered Northeastern University taking four liberal arts courses at night. At the same time, he joined Local 17 for a four-year apprenticeship in the sheet metal business and joined the 513th Maintenance Battalion an army reserve unit. In 1967 he married his high school sweetheart. In 1968 the 513th was activated and the unit was sent to Vietnam as direct support for the One Hundred and First airborne division in northern South Vietnam. Upon returning home Ken first saw his first child and went back to school and the sheet metal business. In 1969 he bought his first house at age 22 and had a second child in 1970. In 1972 he and his wife separated and in 1973 he was laid off from his sheet metal job due to a recession. Soon he was called back to the sheet metal job to draw plans for a school. Ken refused to go back. He told them he would not go back to work unless he knew what he wanted to do. It took three months to decide to become a writer. He began by writing poetry in a notebook and moved on to a novel on an old portable typewriter.

In 1974 a friend showed her husband's boss some of Ken's writing. He loved it and invited Ken to San Francisco where he was given an apartment and a typewriter and told he could finish his novel. The company built and sold bread making kits but also had a small publishing arm. Through the company Ken met a lot of crazy people. Soon the manager came to Ken and said they did not have enough money to publish the book but did Ken know anyone back east who could sell some cocaine. Ken had a cousin connected to the Winter Hill Gang run by Whitey Bolger. Ken called his cousin and the beginning of a deal was set up. While that was all going on the world was being disturbed by the comet Kohoutek which was supposed to be the brightest ever. The cocaine deal never went through and the manager got 6 months in a work camp. Ken decided he could not go home without finishing a book and wrote what he called a mind movie called I MUST TELL and returned to Boston. A month after Ken returned his cousin was murdered by Whitey Bolger.

Back in Boston Ken finished his second mind movie called CAMPBOY in 1976. He could not get the books published and started a publishing house and published them himself. He also wrote a Christmas story told to him by a Christmas tree. He eventually produced it as a plaque and still sells one occasionally. He then started a new novel called KOHOUTEK WAS A BUST about his trip to San Francisco.

Ken is not only a writer. He is also an avid reader. In the seventies he read much about Edgar Cayce, a healer and sear. One could tell or write Cayce a letter about their illness and Cayce would go into a trance and diagnose the illness and tell them what to do about it. In the trance he would also tell people about their past lives. He told many clients they had past lives in the lost continent of Atlantis and what Atlantis was like. He also told them there was evidence of the lost continent at the base of a pyramid in Central America. The chance of finding proof of Atlantis gave Ken an idea and he traveled to Central America in 1976/77 in a quest to find proof of Atlantis. Ken traveled to many pyramids but found no proof until he visited a pyramid in Palenque Mexico. Deep inside the pyramid he found a beautiful carved sarcophagus with a carving of a Mayan flying a rocket ship. He had found his proof.

After his nine-month trip Ken arrived home and got a job picking apples in NH in order to rent a tiny apartment in downtown Boston. There he continued on two more drafts of Kohoutek. In 1979 he took another break from the book and decided he needed the adventure of being a male exotic dancer. He found an agent put together costumes and music and went on the circuit until 1980. He then completed his last draft of KOHOUTEK WAS A BUST. By the time he finished the book he got a small disability for injuries received in Vietnam. With the money he took his two kids and ex-wife around the country for two months and nine thousand miles. When they go home his disability allowed him to go back to school for a degree. Ken spent the next four years at Boston University getting a degree in communications. He graduated in 1985. During his time at BU Ken received a national award for an audio-visual program he produced about his PTSD from Vietnam. He also received a ten thousand dollar grant to write direct and produce an anti-nuke drama which aired on Boston TV. He also met a woman who needed a stripper to advertise her Broadway Babes telegram program on a half hour interview on WBZ in Boston. Ken thought it would be great to sell his books and did a great job in the interview.

In 1984 Ken and his family bought an old fishing lodge in New Hampshire to renovate and turn into a bed and breakfast. Many of his summers than were then used to fix up the fourteen-bedroom house. In 1986 Ken moved to Florida for the winter and bought a small house in WPB and began a children's book called I'M BORED. He also got a night job as a bartender in Palm Beach. When finishing I'M BORED Ken started another novel about his wartime story in Vietnam called KILL A COW. In the summer he was back at what was being called the Inn in NH. Then winter came back south again and so did KILL A COW in Florida.

By 1991 Ken got married again and worked on his novel. Unfortunately, the marriage ended in six months but the novel went on for a few more drafts. In 1998 he got married a third time and bought a new house where he started the novel MAN-DAR OF ATLANTIS. The house was on a lake and Ken observed two birds called moorhens for three years. They acted so human Ken spent two years writing the novel BLACK MENACE about them. He published the novel in 2019. Ken then went back to finishing MAN-DAR OF ATLANTIS, the first book of a MAN-DAR series. He published MAN-DAR in 2021 and is now more than half way through the second book of MAN-DAR called ATLAN.

Kenneth J. Sousa has also traveled the world and lived in several different countries.

Author's website: https://www.kennethjsousa.com